Maud Ballington Boothe

Look up and hope

Maud Ballington Boothe

Look up and hope

ISBN/EAN: 9783337101770

Printed in Europe, USA, Canada, Australia, Japan

Cover: Foto ©Andreas Hilbeck / pixelio.de

More available books at **www.hansebooks.com**

LOOK UP AND HOPE

BY

MRS. BALLINGTON BOOTH

NEW YORK

A. D. F. RANDOLPH COMPANY

1897

LOOK UP AND HOPE.

WHITE lilies raise proudly their graceful heads; buds and blossoms break forth, and to the kiss of sunbeams the little birds twitter as the golden sun casts his first shafts across the sky, and all Nature wakes, while fragrance and song fill the air.

Easter and spring have come to us together, and bring to our hearts thoughts of new life and Heaven-born hope. How welcome is the time of flowers and song-birds, soft breezes and warm sunshine, after the dark, cold hopeless days of winter and the boisterous winds of March !

A writer has said that cold shrivels up the little wings of dreams. I have always disliked winter. It seems indeed a time when dreams and hopes and sweet thoughts were impeded in their flight, and had to bury themselves deep in the heart to keep warm. Leaden skies and chilly fogs, snow, sleet, and rain weigh down not only the atmosphere, but prove often a check to the spirit and a burden to the thoughts; and it is truer still when the surroundings are gloomy, and every effort of will and mind must be exerted to throw off the sad influences.

As the days have grown longer and the sky at even-time has begun to blush with mellow lights, and the coming of birds and flowers have told of the gladness of spring, my heart has bounded, for it has seemed to me that fresh hopes and sweet whiffs of free air and stray beams of golden sunlight would soon be bringing gladdening influences to hearts I love in prison cells. It is impossible to get much into one letter; impossible to write one's heart-thoughts and feelings even in a column or two of print, so I welcome this chance to send some messages to you through the medium of this little booklet, which will be more enduring than a letter, and more personal than notes printed in the "Gazette."

Easter time! After the winter, sweet spring; after the time of frozen brooks and bare, naked trees, fresh singing rivulets and budding green! One seems to speak of death and suffering, the other of life and victory. Look back at what preceded this glad day of hope and life. The Christ of Easter was also the Christ of Calvary. Think of the dark side of the picture: the night of agony in Gethsemane, alone, suffering, forsaken, and betrayed; the trial in which the divine defendant stood arraigned before unjust judge and bitter enemies; sworn against falsely, insulted, condemned amid the acclamations of an incensed mob. Christ the Convict bears His cross up Calvary, bowed with a grief no one can estimate. Christ the Saviour dies in agony, and darkness reigns upon the scene !

The greatest darkness often comes before the dawn, and so the dawn of that first Easter, after the awful scene of Calvary, brought to the world the brightest day-dawn of hope that ever could have come to man. The Christ who looked down on the empty grave that could not hold Him ; the Lord who looked out with love to the dead souls to whom He could bring life ; the world's Redeemer, who passed through the golden gates in company with the thief whom He called to His side in those last moments, — could indeed look back and say, "O Death, where is thy sting! O Grave, where is thy victory!"

The message He sends to sorrowing hearts, the message He would bring to burdened, weary ones still in the dark; the thought that the song of birds and sweetness of flowers lifting their heads to the spring sunshine would whisper over and over again to the messenger-winds this spring-tide is, "Look up and Hope!" To tiny blades of grass pushing their way through the cold ground, the sunbeams said, "Look up and Hope;" and the more they looked up the faster they grew, till the barren brown earth was clothed in their fresh spring verdure. " Look up and Hope," whispered . the wind to the close furled buds on the apple-trees, and they waited and trusted, and now the bare branches are bare no longer, but a mass of snowy whiteness and blushing pink, while busy bees and happy birds rejoice in the fragrance of the blossoms. How could that old knotted tree become so beauti-ful, and the brown earth so soft with its carpet of green? Well, there was some-thing above worth looking to, something worth trusting, even in those early chilly days of spring. From above came the gentle rain and the sweet dew, and more than all the sunshine, warming, cheering, life-giving, and at his touch cold and darkness vanished.

So to the souls dark and dreary, cold and hopeless, comes the message, "Look up and Hope ; " and as they look up they find that comfort and love, sympathy and hope, come from above, and better than all, the dear Sun of Righteousness with healing in His wings and life in His touch looks down in loving response and transforming power.

Sometimes one is tempted to think the night very, very dark, as one looks on the ground, where not an inch of the path can be seen, and into the shadows, so gloomily impenetrable that one can see nothing but blackness; but when one looks up, steadily up to the sky above, star after star shines forth with its message of hope, of infinite might and watchful care. I have heard it said that astronomers have rarely been infidels. The geologist who digs down into the earth, who studies stones and strata, fossils and bones, may become so filled with his theories and dead, dry knowledge, that the instincts of the heart that should turn to the Infinite become petrified, and his mind exalts itself against its Creator and rules out the tender impulses of the heart. With the one who studies the stars, who spends his time watching those worlds upon worlds,

those suns and moons and flying fiery
comets, it is not so. He sees the mighty
ruling controlling power; he feels the
smallness and weakness of human
strength; he stands awed and silenced
before One who is too great to doubt.

But what have stars and budding flowers
and singing birds to do with the hearts in
prison to whom I am writing? Starlit
heavens cannot be very clearly seen from
barred cell windows: budding flowers
will blossom to gladden other eyes, while
their eyes grow weary gazing on bare
walls, and the song-birds do not come to
sing to them, but nest in the far-away
fresh forests amid greenness and freedom
and blossoms. Well, they have just this

much to do with the " boys " in prison. I want their thoughts to fly beyond the bars and walls, and gather from these hopeful, brighter things in life the lesson of comfort they can bring. Pure thoughts are like the bees that leave the hive and fly hither and thither, gathering honey from clover and rose, or from myrtle and honeysuckle, and come back with their precious store to enrich the comb. Hopeless, evil thoughts are ever flying back into the shadow of the night, and like the bat, they seek the darkest corners and hide from the pure, sweet sunlight.

But what have stars, flowers, and birds to do with you, did I ask? Well, I think the stars can speak of hope, — strong true inspired hope, that lifts us from our hopeless little selves, up, up to God, and they tell us that for us in our once dark sky He has Himself placed gleams of heavenly light. Flowers pure and fragrant bring their message of new life, — a life that can be pure and beautiful; a life that can not only be lived above the stain and corruption that would tend to spoil it, but a life that can be lived for others, — for no flower blossoms for itself alone. Then do not the songs of birds speak of gladness of heart, of joy, of victory, such as can come to the soul alone who has been made free by the love of Christ, and filled with the dear spirit which He can shed abroad within it?

Sometimes the clouds of past failure and sorrow hang so low and prove so impenetrable as to make it hard to believe that there is any star shining behind the clouds for them. The awful past is so dark and vivid in its haunting memories, that it not only blights the present and shuts out the comforting star-gleams, but it sends forth its gloomy shadows to overcast the future, and like a dread nightmare it rises and blocks every avenue to which the longing thoughts would turn for relief. The past is dead if you will but believe it; let it die indeed this Easter-tide, and from its grave let sweet Hope arise, pure and fragrant as the flower from the earth. Past failures, disappointments, and sins must not prove the chilly frost that will blight the buds of promise; must not blow like the cold chill winds to shrivel the little wings of sweeter dreams. Rather let them do their work and prove to us the lessons that will make the future stronger, brighter, and better. Trees are fertilized by their own dead leaves and branches; the wind comes and shakes from the tree its seared, yellow leaves; the winter comes and breaks away the tangled branches; and as they lay down around its roots they sink into the soil, so that it can often be said that the forest rises and throws up into the air its glad, green branches, gaining strength from the losses of the past.   So let it be with the losses and failures of *your* past !   They have been sinful, dark, and hopeless, but from this experience you can draw lessons which will make the future brighter than it ever otherwise could have been.   From the wasted hours and the many errors of a sinful life, new hopes and brave resolves may spring, chasing the memory of the past and reaching out to the hopes of the future.

Yesterday now is a part of forever;
  Bound up in a sheaf which God holds tight,
With glad days, and sad days, and bad days
    which never
  Shall visit us more with their bloom or their
    blight,
  Their fulness of sunshine or sorrowful night.

Let them go since we cannot relieve them.
Cannot undo and cannot atone ;
God in his mercy receive, forgive them !
Only the new days are our own.
To-day is ours, and to-day alone.

When we leave the past we naturally look into the future. To some it holds nothing, to others a delusive prospect ; and yet to all it may hold, if they will but see it, a true strong gleam of *hope*.

While crossing the desert in California in the fall of last year I looked up from my writing and saw gleaming in the distance a beautiful silvery lake. Amid that arid country, composed of alkali desert, bare rocks, and grey sage-bush, it was indeed a welcome sight as it lay, calm and bright, reflecting the rocks and hills on its placid breast. I thought how the weary travellers who crossed that stretch of country in the pioneer days must have welcomed the sight of it. "What lake is that?" I asked the porter. "Lake! Why, that's no lake," he answered disdainfully, "it is only a mirage." As I watched the cruel, deceptive waters that falsely shimmered where in reality was only arid sand, I thought of the despair just such a sight had often brought to the thirsty, fainting traveller. So are often self-made plans, worldly ambitions, earthly affections, bright, promising, and hopeful as they may seem to the weary longing heart and struggling empty life that reaches out to grasp them. But alas! they fade and

vanish, and leave the one who has followed so hard after them weary, discour-
aged, and sick at heart.

The hope that Christ gives is one so
sweet, so lasting, so inspiring, that those
who have followed its gleam have found
that it pointed as unmistakably to LIFE
as the Star of Bethlehem did to the Christ-
babe's manger, — new, glad, risen *life*,
before which the darkness flies away
and tears are lighted with a rainbow
glory.

Life ! What a wonderful word that is
in counter-distinction to the word Death,
with all its thoughts of cold, stiff helpless-
ness and its awful irrevocableness. A
worm has eaten its way to the roots of

your plant and blighted it; its fresh, green leaves are limp and yellow; the stems are shrivelled, and the flowers droop, and the little buds which will never now unfold, drop off, and soon it stands a lifeless, sapless thing, worthless and un-sightly.

You take tenderly from the grass the little songster who has fallen, pierced by a cruel shot; the eyes grow dim, and the little head falls limply from side to side; the wings lie helpless as you stretch them out, feather by feather. No longer will that little throat be filled with song-joy; never again will those pinions soar up, up towards Heaven. Life has gone, and nothing is left but the poor little feathered body, soon to become a prey to the insect world of a lower order.

Have we not all sat by the bedside of some loved one after the spirit has flown; pressed the cold hand from which no answering touch was felt; called the dear name in an agony of grief, but to receive no answer from the still lips? Death! death in the physical world is an awful thing, — so real, so cold, so inevitable, so impossible to change or overcome, that its thought has become a dread to all living things, and its approach casts a dark shadow that hushes mirth and robs the sunlight of its very brightness.

What about death in the spiritual world?

It cannot be quite so clearly discerned by the onlooker, does not seem so awful to the world because it does not affect the sight, hearing, touch, or other senses ; but in reality it does affect not only the life to come, but the present. We cannot go to our work or pleasures, meet our sorrows, carry our cares, or plan our future with a dead soul within us without its condition being a constant menace to our temporal safety, and without its having a deep, marked influence upon our thoughts, actions, and character. A soul deaf to God's voice is very easily charmed by the voice of the tempter. An eye blind to the purity and righteousness of a Christ-following life and to the claims of its

Saviour looks all too keenly and longingly on evil, and the pride of life, and on those things that can but curse and blight where they are followed. A heart that answers not to the great love divine, that has been cold and hard, that has shut itself against tender pleadings and earnest prayers, is soil prepared indeed for all the seeds and influences of evil that can be cast into it by the enemy of man's soul. Such a heart may readily break human law and lay aside human ideas of rectitude and honor, because it has in it no power to control, no life to inspire.

But when we speak of poor, dead souls we need not speak hopelessly as we do when the physical life is gone out.

The bird, the flower, the loved human body lie helpless, and we can only hide them away under the green mother-earth that will cover and enfold them; but in the spiritual world all is different. There, the risen Lord, the Conqueror of all death, and the One at whose touch the young man of Nain arose, at the sound of whose voice Lazarus came forth, stands ready and waiting to bring back life, and *that* life everlasting. The Hand that gave the touch of healing to the leper, brought sight to the blind, and made the lame to walk; that thrust back, at its stretching forth, disease and death itself, is just as powerful, just as tender, just as near to help to-day as ever it was in the days of old, and the Christ-hand brings in its touch LIFE. How strange and wonderful has this new life seemed to some of you who have already found it ! The old desires, old temptations, and old habits that seemed so absolutely unconquerable as to become ruling powers in your life, have vanished like shadows before the sunlight. Yesterday they were chains that wrapped in grim slavery your poor heart, — to-day they lie in broken fragments at your feet, and you look down upon them with a song of triumph on your lips. What your own poor hands could never have accomplished, what your own resolutions and efforts would have failed in breaking, has been done by the divine power that brings in deliverance and transformation with its entrance. Now you know full well that I believe in the possibility of this wonderful new life, coming to those who are shut in prison cells, as truly as it can come to those in happy homes and costly churches, who have never known the shame and sorrow of prison life. For my part I am inclined to believe from what I have learned of the Christ-heart that the dear Life-giver would sooner go to the souls that need Him most, and that where the blight of sin has fallen the heaviest, and the reaping has been the most bitter, He would hasten the more eagerly to bring His tender, compassionate touch to the heart that is hopeless, forsaken, and crushed. He stands ever waiting and longing to enter in, that He may banish the night and bring the Easter dawn of a new, glad, holy life to just such souls. I know many prison cells that are now brightened by His presence, and many, many hearts beating, still, it's true, beneath the stripes, and yet beating with glad, new feelings and a joy that dark surroundings cannot shut out. So is it a wonder that my message this Easter time to all that read these few pages is an earnest plea for them to seek the loving, living, personal Saviour who can do so much for them? Often do I quote to those who seem to

be groping in a half dawn, battling their
weary way through the clouds and mist,
those strong, true lines that speak of
Christ the Saviour as He is : —

Reality ! Reality !
Lord Jesus Christ, Thou art to me.
From the spectral mists and driving clouds,
From the shifting shadows and phantom crowds,
From unreal worlds and unreal lives
Where truth with falsehood feebly strives,
From the passing away, the chance and change,
Flickerings, vanishings, swift and strange, —
I turn to my glorious rest on Thee,
Who art the grand Reality.

Reality in greatest need ;
Lord Jesus Christ, Thou art indeed.
Is the pilot real who alone can guide
The drifting ship through midnight tide ?
Is the life-boat real as it nears the wreck,
And the saved ones leap from the parting deck ?

Is the haven real where the barque may flee
From the autumn gales of the wild North sea?
Reality indeed art Thou,
My Pilot, Life-boat, Haven now.

But as we speak of LIFE, other thoughts
crowd into my mind.   Life is not given
for selfish ends.   No flower, no creature,
no being, has ever been created or
ordained by God to live for itself alone,
nor are good gifts given to be enjoyed or
shut up within the heart of the one who
receives them.   The snows melt, the
rains fall, and, drop by drop, stream by
stream, the living, singing, rippling tor-
rent gains its strength gladly and joyfully.
It runs down the mountain side, through
the forest, along the meadow, away, away,

ever downward and onward towards the river and the sea. Always receiving, it is always giving. Its waters are clear and fresh and sparkling, because it keeps them not for itself. Standing away up on the mountain where you cannot see the stream, you can yet trace its course, for the grass is greener, the trees are stronger, and the whole country is brightened by its passing through. Cattle quench their thirst; little birds stoop and drink in its freshness, and it comes to all as a reviving blessing. Look at the contrast. The pool that receives the rain and has no outlet, gives nothing to others, so the water which was once clear and sweet becomes polluted, stagnant, while slimy scum gathers upon its dark breast. Myriads and myriads of noxious fermentations spread disease and danger to the swamp around it. It has seemed to me that some hearts are like the living spring, while other selfish souls are like the stagnant pond. God gave to both at first, but one has gladly given out to others, and to that one an ever-fresh supply has come ; but to the other selfish, stagnant experiences comes misery, for they have lost themselves that which might have been so precious to them and to others.

The life that Christ can bring to the heart He enters must be a life that can be "read and known of all men," as pure, strong, true, and victorious !

When the spring comes you know it: flowers and leaves, song-birds and sunbeams proclaim it; and so it is with the life upon which the Sun of Righteousness has risen. You can no more keep it from the knowledge of the world around than you can hide the results of springtime in the forest. But what a miserable, cold, stiff, unlovely thing religion seems to be from some people's rendering of it! Religion is not a creed or belief; not something which we are to accept and tack on to our life to make it respectable; not a performing of some duties and an acceptance of some obligations. Religion, if it is anything, is *life*, — new life coming into the soul, as truly as spring comes into

Nature, making all things new; and it is this kind of religion and this alone that can bring victory to the soul, peace to the heart, and constant strength to the one whose good resolutions and efforts would otherwise prove so fruitless and discouragingly weak.

Victory! What a ringing, cheering word that is! Oh, how much it means to weary, hard-pressed warriors who have toiled and suffered bravely, faced the foe and stood the storm of shot and shell! Victory is sweet because it has always meant a battle to gain it. As the cheer rises and falls in notes of joy upon the calm, still air, it is all the gladder and fuller because it takes the place of the crash and thunder of tumult and strife. Souls that most truly rejoice to-day in the calm and rest of the peace that Christ can bring, know full well what a storm and struggle, what a conflict with doubts and fears, and what a battle with self preceded that entrance of light into their hearts. A great general among the ancients, when urged to cease from the wars and struggles with the foes of his State, that they might enjoy a season of peace, answered tersely, " Pax paritur bello," — " Peace is born of war ! " Truly in things spiritual it can be said that peace, the true, deep, lasting peace of the soul, is only born after the battle has been fought out and gained ; the foe not parleyed with, but conquered; the wrong mastered, and the right enthroned. Oh, the fallacy of soothing a guilty conscience; oh, the danger of crying peace, peace, where there is no peace; oh, the pity of saying to the soul, "ONLY believe on the Lord Jesus Christ," when the conscience rises up and shows that heart, that something is necessary before any belief can bring peace.

There are some who will seek peace, but who will not pay the cost. They want the sense of sins pardoned, of a guilty conscience stilled, of safety for the future; but they are too cowardly to fight the matter out, to face and deal with them-

selves, their doubts, their allowed wrong-
doings. They want the flag of victory
hoisted and the reign of peace proclaimed
in the citadel, but they are not ready to
have the enemy cast out or the evil guest
slain. They parley; they want half and
half measures; they would hold to the
skirts of the King of Righteousness with
one hand for fear He will forsake them,
but they still hold tight to the things they
have liked and followed after with the
other. This will always prove a failure,
a miserable defeat. It cannot be otherwise.

When the dear Christ-life enters in,
when the soul lays down its arms of
rebellion, the Lord himself casts out the

enemies and brings in a power that not only saves, but keeps the soul. There is then an influence within that can enable the Christ-follower to meet each difficulty, to face each temptation, to go through each battle, and yet to be ever victorious. The glad song of triumph and joy can go up from the heart as naturally and as constantly as the songs of the little bird in the sunshine, for the new life is a risen life indeed, that has within it a power far exceeding human effort or courage or determination. Life in the natural world is a struggle against disease, danger, and death; life in the spiritual world is a fight against sin and evil, and soul-spoiling influences. No one can enter into the new life and make a success of it who thinks he can easily and effortlessly drift onward to a haven of rest on calm seas without struggle or sacrifice. Christ-following while in this world will always mean a warfare, and it is only those who will fight the good fight of faith, who will finish their course with songs of victory. But is it not those very struggles, those very battles for the resisting of evil and the advance in a new life, that bring with strengthening of character brave purposes, and a daily growth in grace? The finest, strongest trees are not those hidden away in sheltered nooks, but the tall pines and firs of the mountain side, where the strong winds sweep. They are tempered, tested, and strengthened by their battle with the storm, and it is they that attain the strongest, noblest growth.

Many of you are where you are to-day because you yielded to the tide instead of battling against it. As you look back upon the past you can see point after point where you weakened your own character for want of the courage to stand up and brave the storm. You could have strengthened your character, but instead you just drifted, and that drifting weakened you, and every battle lost proved a further sapping away of its strength. But this must not make you hopeless. Let it rather strengthen and inspire you to valiant efforts in the future. I know and understand you as perhaps very few can, for have I not, since God sent me to you, entered into your lives and learned to love you? And I, who know many of your difficulties, temptations, and suffering, and something of what awaits you when you step out again into the world, can tell you that I am gaining fresh hope each day, and feel a stronger confidence that thousands of you are coming forth into the world new men in Christ Jesus, so that old things may indeed pass away and all things become new. The outside world has been discussing theories, collecting statistics, for years, upon what it calls "the criminal problem." They have written papers and given learned discourses upon the question, "Can the Criminal be Reclaimed?" I turn to you and say that the problem lies in your hands, not theirs. The men who will turn to the Power from above that can make them strong, pure, brave, and victorious, can come out a great army of resolute souls who shall prove by their future how truly the past can be redeemed; and the path they make through the difficulties and obstacles which must, for a time, face them, will make it all the easier for the many feet that will in the future follow them.

God bless you! I cannot look at the flowers of spring, I cannot listen to the singing of birds, I cannot see the glad sunshine, without praying for you in the darkness of your prison cell. All life is changed to me since I learned to love you, and into the very depth of my soul the mother's yearning over you has grown day by day. My life is yours, and if by word of lip or pen, by work or sacrifice, I can help you, you can always rely on me as your true friend who cares and understands about your present and your future.

www.ingramcontent.com/pod-product-compliance
Lightning Source LLC
Chambersburg PA
CBHW061236260626
47172CB00003B/884